# THE *Princess* IN
# BLACK
## and the PERFECT PRINCESS PARTY

## Shannon Hale & Dean Hale

*illustrated by*
## LeUyen Pham

SCHOLASTIC INC.

ISBN 978-1-338-11281-8

Text copyright © 2015 by Shannon and Dean Hale.
Illustrations copyright © 2015 by LeUyen Pham.
All rights reserved. Published by Scholastic Inc.,
557 Broadway, New York, NY 10012, by arrangement with
Candlewick Press. SCHOLASTIC and associated logos are
trademarks and/or registered trademarks of Scholastic Inc.

12 11 10 9 8 7 6 5 4 3 2 1          16 17 18 19 20 21

Printed in the U.S.A.          40

This edition first printing, September 2016

This book was typeset in Kennerly.
The illustrations were done in watercolor and ink.

# *Chapter 1*

Pink balloons topped the castle towers. Pink balloons bobbed from the treetops. There was even a pink balloon tied to a unicorn's horn.

Today was Princess Magnolia's birthday. She wanted the party to be perfect.

Princess Magnolia cleaned her tower room. She put on her favorite fluffy dress. She polished her glass slippers. She frosted cupcakes.

She looked out her window. Her guests would arrive any moment.

And then her glitter-stone ring rang.

"The monster alarm," said Princess Magnolia. "Not now!"

It was time for Princess Magnolia's birthday party. It was not a good time for a monster attack.

# Chapter 2

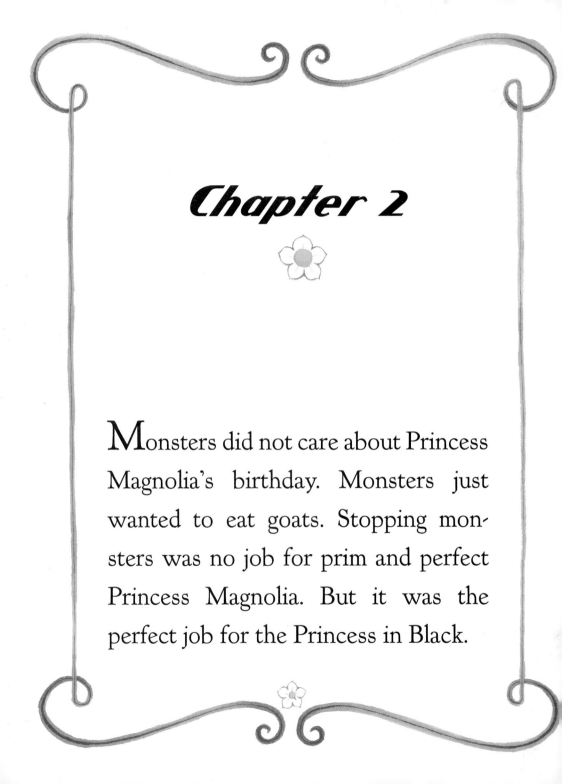

Monsters did not care about Princess Magnolia's birthday. Monsters just wanted to eat goats. Stopping monsters was no job for prim and perfect Princess Magnolia. But it was the perfect job for the Princess in Black.

Princess Magnolia ducked into the broom closet.

She took off her favorite fluffy dress.
She slipped off her glass slippers.

Underneath, she was dressed all in black. She fastened on her mask.

She was no longer Princess Magnolia.
She was the Princess in Black.

"The princess is back!" said the
Princess in Black.

She slid down the secret chute.

She high-jumped the castle wall.

Twelve sparkly princesses were riding toward the drawbridge. Her party guests!

She hoped they wouldn't look up. No one knew that prim and perfect Princess Magnolia was also the Princess in Black.

# *Chapter 3*

No one knew the Princess in Black's secret identity, except her faithful steed. He was a steed with his own secret.

Everyone thought that Frimplepants was a unicorn. After all, he had a horn on his head. Today a pink balloon was tied to his horn. For the party.

When Frimplepants pranced, the balloon bobbed. When Frimplepants cantered, the balloon swayed. Frimplepants was in a festive mood.

That is, until his glitter-stone horseshoe rang. The monster alarm!

Frimplepants went into a secret passage.

When he came out the other side, he was no longer Frimplepants the unicorn. He was Blacky, the Princess in Black's faithful pony!

Blacky went to the usual place beside the castle wall. He waited for the Princess in Black to land on his back.

Blacky was ready to fight monsters! But he kind of missed the balloon.

# Chapter 4

The Princess in Black landed on Blacky's back.

"Fly, Blacky, fly!" she said.

Blacky could not fly. He was a pony. He was not a Pegasus. But he knew that when the Princess in Black said "fly" she really meant "run fast." And so Blacky ran fast.

They zoomed through the forest.

Duff the goat boy watched over the grazing goats. He did not notice a tentacle creeping out of a nearby hole. More tentacles followed. A monster rose up.

"Help!" Duff said.

The Princess in Black rode into the goat pasture.

"BLEAT BOATS!" the monster gurgled.

"Huh?" said Duff.

"Huh?" said the Princess in Black.

The monster lifted a tentacle to its mouth. It coughed horribly.

"EAT GOATS!" the monster shrieked.

"Ah," said Duff.

"Ah," said the Princess in Black.

All monsters were the same. They only wanted to eat goats. They did not care about a princess's birthday.

The Princess in Black pushed a switch on her scepter. It turned into a staff.

"Behave, beast!" she shouted. "Back to Monster Land."

"NO! EAT GOATS!" it said.

So the tentacled monster and the
Princess in Black waged battle.

FRIMPLE
FLIP! ✿

ROYAL
WRANGLE! ✿

The monster went back into the hole. They always did. Eventually. "Hooray!" said Duff.

The Princess in Black waved. She and her pony raced back to the castle.

Moments later, Princess Magnolia came out of the broom closet. Her hair was a little messy.

She ran down the stairs. She opened the castle door.

"Happy Birthday!" shouted
the twelve sparkly princesses.

# Chapter 5

Princess Magnolia was having a wonderful time. The sandwiches were delicious. The tablecloths were fancy. The princesses were delightful. It was a perfect party.

"Open the presents!" said Princess Snapdragon.

"Yes, do!" said the other eleven princesses.

Princess Magnolia clapped her hands. She could hardly wait.

"Oh, thank you!" she said. "Presents make a party particularly perfect."

Just then, her glitter-stone ring rang.

It was time to open presents. It was not a good time for a monster attack.

"What is that ringing noise?" asked Princess Snapdragon.

"It's an alarm," said Princess Magnolia.

She couldn't tell them it was the monster alarm. Then they might guess that she was the Princess in Black. No one knew she was the Princess in Black. (Except Blacky, of course.)

"That alarm means it's . . . time for a game!" said Princess Magnolia.

"Yay!" said Princess Bluebell. "What game should we play?"

"Um, how about hide-and-seek?" said Princess Magnolia. "Not It!"

Princess Tulip was It. She counted.
The princesses sneaked away.

Princess Honeysuckle hid under a table.

Princess Crocus hid behind the bathroom door.

Princess Magnolia hid in the broom closet.

# Chapter 6

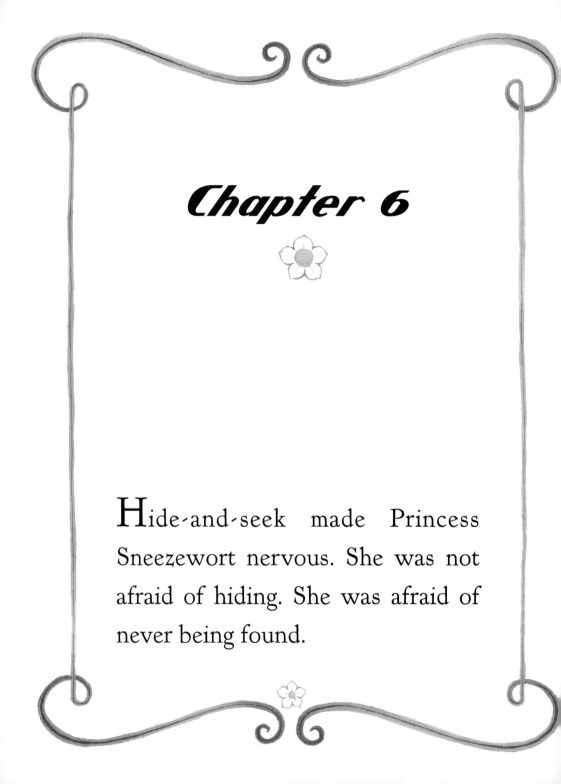

Hide-and-seek made Princess Sneezewort nervous. She was not afraid of hiding. She was afraid of never being found.

Princess Sneezewort blended in with the drapes.

Princess Sneezewort blended in with the table lamps.

Princess Sneezewort blended in with the rug.

Princess Tulip walked by. But she did not notice Princess Sneezewort.

Princess Sneezewort sighed. She was lonely. The rug wasn't very good company.

She had seen Princess Magnolia hide in the broom closet. She would follow. At least then she wouldn't have to hide alone.

Princess Sneezewort opened the closet. There was Princess Magnolia's fluffy dress. There were her glass slippers. But there was no Princess Magnolia.

"That's curious," said Princess Sneezewort. "Where did she go?"

# Chapter 7

The Princess in Black was back in the goat pasture. Normally, fighting monsters was a pleasant way to pass an afternoon. But today she wanted to open presents.

"Behave, beast!" she said.

"NO! EAT GOATS!" said the scaly monster.

The Princess in Black sighed.
Monsters could be so exasperating.
When would they learn? She would
*not* let them eat the goats!

The Princess in Black and the scaly
monster waged battle.

SCEPTER SPANK!

PASTURE DASH!

TWINKLE TWINKLE LITTLE

SMASH!

The monster went back to Monster
Land. They always did. Eventually.

The Princess in Black raced back to the castle.

She crawled back up the chute.

She pulled on the fluffy dress. She slipped on the glass slippers.

"Where did you come from?" said a voice.

Princess Magnolia froze.

# *Chapter 8*

Princess Magnolia was not alone in the broom closet.

"Who's there?" asked Princess Magnolia.

"It's me. Princess Sneezewort."

Princess Magnolia squinted. All she saw were some brooms.

The brooms moved.

"Wow, Princess Sneezewort," she said. "You blended in with the brooms. You're really good at hiding."

"So are you," said Princess Sneezewort. "I've been in this closet for an hour. I saw your dress. I didn't think you were in it."

The closet door opened.

"I found you!" said Princess Tulip. "You two are good hiders. I checked this closet three times."

"That is curious," said Princess Sneezewort.

# Chapter 9

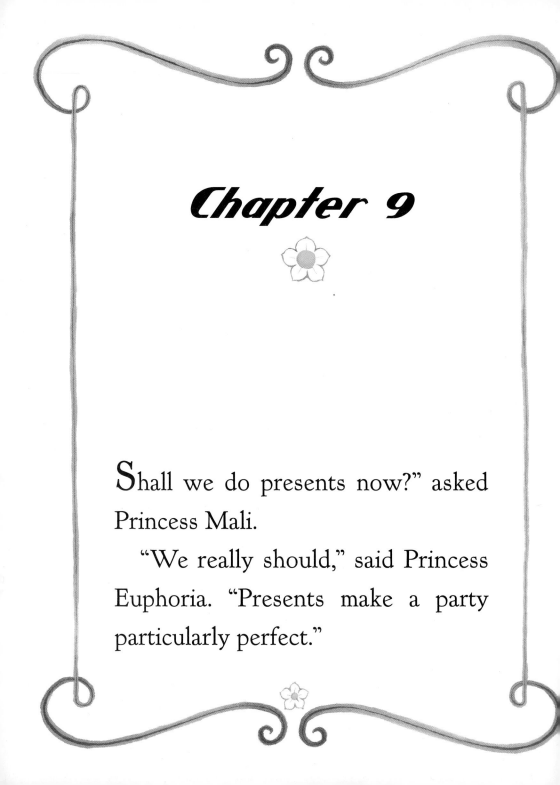

Shall we do presents now?" asked Princess Mali.

"We really should," said Princess Euphoria. "Presents make a party particularly perfect."

"Oh, goody!" said Princess Magnolia.
There was a ringing sound.

"What is that noise?" asked Princess
Orchid.

"It's the alarm again," said Princess
Magnolia. She sighed. "Um . . . it's time
for the races."

The princesses went outside. The princesses mounted their mounts. Ready, set, go!

Princess Magnolia and her unicorn, Frimplepants, won the first race.

Princess Sneezewort and her pig,
Sir Hogswell, came in last.

There was a second race. Princess Bluebell and her Pegasus, Jollybuck, won.

Princess Sneezewort and Sir Hogswell came in last.

There was a third race. Princess
Zinnia and her stag, Santa Bear, won.

There was a fourth race. Princess
Apple Blossom and her antelope, Ed,
won.

Princess Sneezewort was always last. Sir Hogswell did not believe in races. Sir Hogswell did not believe in speed. Sir Hogswell believed in dinner, dessert, and a good night's sleep.

From the back, Princess Sneezewort could see all the princesses. She could see all their mounts. But she could no longer see Princess Magnolia and Frimplepants.

There was a fifth race. That time, Princess Magnolia came in last. She rode up behind Princess Sneezewort. Her hair was messy. Her glass slippers were on the wrong feet.

"That is curious," said Princess Sneezewort.

# *Chapter 10*

Now is it time for presents?" asked
Princess Apple Blossom.

"I hope so," said Princess Magnolia.
"Because presents make a party—"

The ringing noise interrupted her.

"Another alarm?" asked Princess Sneezewort.

"Yes…" Princess Magnolia frowned. "It's time to do . . . the maze! We can open presents after. I promise."

The princesses entered the garden maze.

Princess Sneezewort got lost.
She thought she would be
the last one out.

Eventually she found the exit. Eleven princesses were waiting. But one more was still in the maze.

Finally Princess Magnolia emerged. Her hair was even messier. Her dress was inside out.

"That is remarkably curious," said Princess Sneezewort.

# Chapter 11

"Now is it time for presents?" asked Princess Euphoria.

"Um . . ." said Princess Magnolia.

She held her breath. She listened. She looked at her ring. No ringing.

"Yes!" she said. "It really is time for presents."

The princesses went back to the tower. They sat on sofas. Princess Hyacinth handed Princess Magnolia the first gift.

It felt heavy and round. Could it be a racing helmet? A goldfish bowl? A crystal ball? Princess Magnolia couldn't wait to see!

Then something happened. Something that made Princess Magnolia want to cry.

Her glitter-stone ring rang.

It was really, really time for presents. It was a really, really bad time for a monster attack.

"Does that alarm mean it's time for presents?" asked Princess Honeysuckle.

Princess Magnolia whimpered.

"Please stay here," she said. "I'll be right back. I promise."

# Chapter 12

Princess Magnolia left her tower room. She sneaked into the broom closet again. She changed her clothes again.

She went down the chute. She high-jumped the castle wall. Blacky was waiting. She landed on his back. They rode through the forest. They galloped into the goat pasture. Again.

Yet another monster was terrorizing the goats. A pink monster this time.

"ROOAARR!" it said. "EAT GOAT—"

"No!" said the Princess in Black. "No eating goats. I don't want to fight any more monsters today! I have had it. It's my BIRTHDAY. And it's time for PRESENTS. Do you hear me? I said, IT'S TIME FOR PRESENTS!"

# Chapter 13

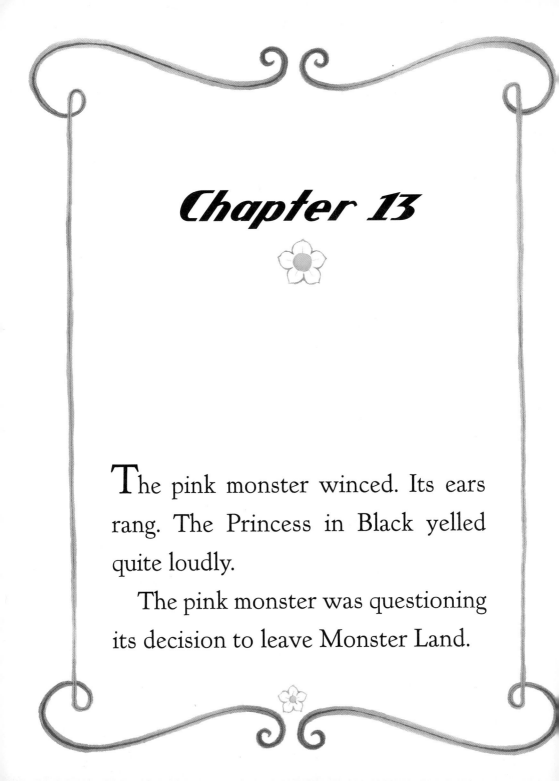

The pink monster winced. Its ears rang. The Princess in Black yelled quite loudly.

The pink monster was questioning its decision to leave Monster Land.

Sure, Monster Land had no goats.
But it also had no yelling princesses.

Now things were awkward. It seemed today was the Princess in Black's birthday. She was expecting presents. And the pink monster hadn't brought a thing.

It checked its pockets. Oh, goody! Stones! Pink stones it had found in a cave. There were twelve of them. They would have to do.

The pink monster held out the stones. The pink monster cleared its throat.

"HAPPY BIRTHDAY!"
it roared politely.

# Chapter 14

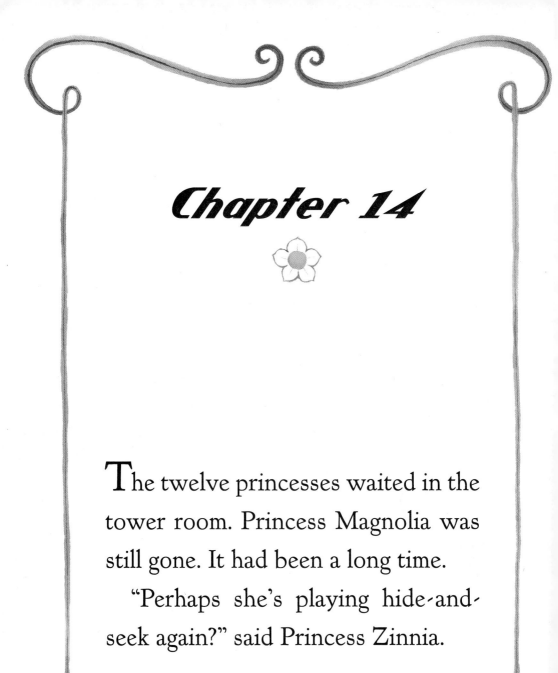

The twelve princesses waited in the tower room. Princess Magnolia was still gone. It had been a long time.

"Perhaps she's playing hide-and-seek again?" said Princess Zinnia.

They searched the castle. No Princess Magnolia.

"Maybe she's in the broom closet," said Princess Sneezewort. "She was in there last time."

They went to the broom closet. Princess Sneezewort reached for the door handle.

Just then, Princess Magnolia came out. Her hair was extremely messy. Her dress was inside out and backward. One of her glass slippers was missing.

"Princess Magnolia, you keep disappearing," said Princess Sneezewort. "Every time it's time for presents."

"I do?" said Princess Magnolia.

"Yes, you do," said Princess Sneezewort. "Don't you want presents? Where do you keep going?"

Princess Magnolia looked down. Her hands were full of stones. She held them up.

"To get presents for you!" she said. "After all, presents make a party particularly perfect."

She handed out the stones. There was one for each princess. They were clear and pink and very pretty.

"They're perfect!" said Princess Sneezewort. "Absolutely perfect."

It all was. The company. The games. The gifts. It was the most perfect party Princess Magnolia had ever had.